The Littlest Cock
Copyright © 2017 by Antonio Carter

MW01489485

THE LITTLEST COCK MADE A DRAMATIC EXIT! NOT THAT THE PUSSIES CARED.

"GLAD, THAT'S DONE." HE HEARD AS HE WAS LEAVING.

"IT DIDN'T WORK,"
THE LITTLEST COCK COMPLAINED,
"THE PUSSIES LET ME PLAY
BUT THEY DIDN'T LIKE ME.
I THINK THEY WANTED
TO PLAY WITH
A BIGGER COCK."

"PROBABLY,"
SAID THE BIG DOG.
"WHY DON'T YOU TRY
PLAYING WITH THE ASSES?
THEY'RE USUALLY OPEN TO
ACCEPTING
NEWCOMERS
BUT THEY CAN BE
REALLY MESSY."

"THE ASSES?"
QUESTIONED THE
LITTLEST COCK,
"I NEVER THOUGHT
ABOUT THEM...
I DON'T MIND THEIR MESSINESS
BUT HOW DO I GET
THEM TO PLAY WITH ME?"

HE SENT THE ASSES A VERY IMPRESSIVE PICTURE...
BUT IT WASN'T A PICTURE OF HIM.
IT WAS A PICTURE OF A MUCH BIGGER COCK.
A BIG BLACK COCK TO BE EXACT.

THE LITTLEST COCK STARED AT THE MASTER BAIT WITH ASTONISHMENT. IT WAS INCREDIBLY BEAUTIFUL. HE ACCEPTED THE GIFT GRACIOUSLY, AND THE CATFISH WARNED HIM:

"LITTLE COCK BE WARNED: KEEPING THE MASTER BAIT TOO LONG COULD CAUSE DIRE CONSEQUENCES. PLAYING ALONE IS IMPORTANT, BUT WHEN DONE TOO LONG IT CAN MAKE YOU FORGET THE BEAUTY OF COMPANIONSHIP. AT SOME POINT, YOU MUST PASS THE MASTER BAIT ON TO SOME OTHER LITTLE COCK IN NEED, FOR YOUR SAKE AND THEIRS."

"BUT HOW WILL I KNOW WHEN TO PASS IT ON?" ASKED THE LITTLEST COCK.

"YOU WILL KNOW WHEN THE TIME COMES!" AND WITH THAT THE MAJESTIC CATFISH VANISHED.

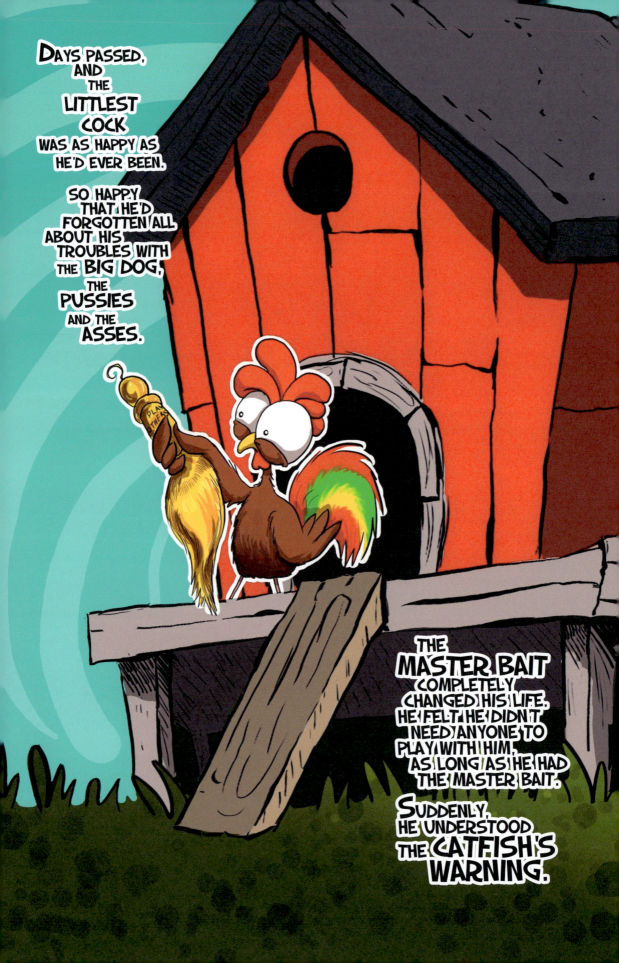

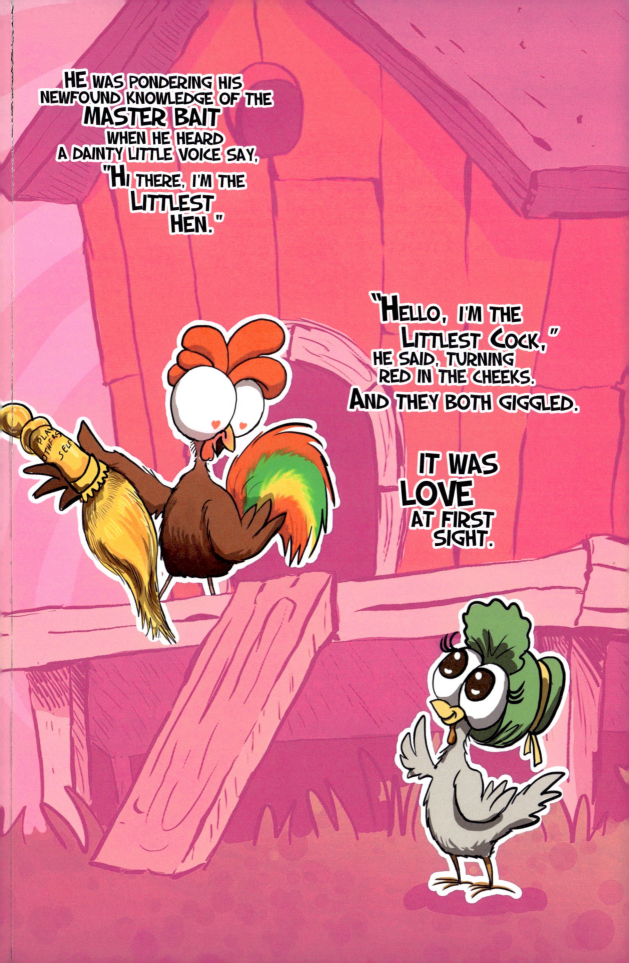

Made in the USA
Columbia, SC
21 May 2025

58259820R00027